Buster

The Very Shy Dog

by Lisze Bechtold

Houghton Mifflin Company
Boston

For Allen, William, Austin, and Beau

Copyright © 1999 by Lisze Bechtold

www.houghtonmifflinbooks.com

Library of Congress Cataloging-in-Publication Data

Bechtold, Lisze.
Buster, the very shy dog / Lisze Bechtold.
p. cm.
Summary: In three stories, Buster the dog overcomes his shyness to make a friend,
discovers his special talent, and helps Phoebe find the garbage bandits.
RNF ISBN 0-395-85008-8 PAP ISBN 0-618-11122-0
[1. Dogs — Fiction. 2. Bashfulness — Fiction.] I. Title.
PZ7.B380765Bu 1999   97-12452
[E] — dc21   CIP   AC

Manufactured in the United States of America
BVG 10 9 8 7 6 5 4 3

CONTENTS

Buster's First Party

When Buster first came to Roger's house,
he was small and shy.

Phoebe, Roger's other dog, was not shy.
She was bossy.

The cats were bossy, too.

When Buster grew up, he was big and shy,
but he still felt small.

When someone came to visit,
Buster would run and hide.
Most people met Buster by accident.

One day a lot of people came to visit.
It was hard for Buster to find a place to hide.

"A party!" barked Phoebe.
"Roger's birthday party!"
"What is a party?" wondered Buster.
He watched as Phoebe made new friends
and helped herself to ice cream and cake.
"I wish I could have some ice cream and cake too,"
thought Buster, "but someone might see me."

When everyone went outside
to watch Phoebe do her fancy tricks,
Buster crept out from behind the couch.

He looked at the ice cream and cake.
He smelled the ice cream and cake.
He almost tasted the ice cream and cake.

But then someone shouted,
"Hey, look! Another dog! Can he do tricks, too?"

Buster ran and hid again,
until a little girl saw him.
"Here, doggy, doggy," she yelled.

Soon a long line of kids was following
Buster around and around the house.
"Here, doggy, doggy!" called the little girl.
"HERE, DOGGY, DOGGY!" called all the other kids.

Buster slipped under the back porch.
"I don't think I like parties," he sighed,
"except for the ice cream and cake."

After a while, Buster heard a sniffle,
then a little sob.
He peeked out.
When a little girl looked down at him,
Buster backed far away.

"Now she will say, 'Here, doggy, doggy,'" he thought.
But the girl did not say anything.
She just sat and cried.

Buster watched her
for a long time.

He wanted her to feel better,
but he did not know what to do.

Then Buster did something very brave.

After a while the girl talked to him.
"I don't know anyone at this party.
No one played with me.
Then that other dog ate all
of my ice cream and cake!"

Buster knew just how she felt.
"You are a nice dog," she said,
"much nicer than that other one.
Wait here." She ran into the house.
When she came back, the little girl said,
"Let's have ice cream and cake!"

Buster and Phoebe

Buster thought Phoebe was an amazing dog.
Phoebe was brave.

She was good at finding things.

Most of all,
she was an ace ball catcher.
She could catch any ball,
no matter how far

or how high
Roger threw it.
"Good dog, Phoebe!"
Roger always said.

"Every dog should be able to catch,"
Phoebe told Buster. "You just have to
keep your eye on the ball."
Buster tried keeping his eye on the ball.

It did not help.
"Phoebe is good at everything," he thought,
"and I'm not good at anything."

"I have an idea," said Phoebe. "Follow me."
She picked up her ball and ran to Roger's room.

"Maybe you need glasses," she said, "like Roger."

But glasses did not help.

The hamster cage crashed to the floor.
Roger woke up.
"Oh no!" he cried. "Where's Maxie?"

Roger looked all around the room for Maxie the hamster.

Phoebe sniffed all around the room for Maxie.

Buster slunk toward the door.
"I'm not good at finding things," he thought.

Phoebe gave up sniffing.
Roger flopped down on the bed.
"I've had Maxie ever since the fourth grade," he said.
"What if she is lost forever?"
Buster rested his chin on Roger's arm.

Roger sighed deeply. Buster sighed, too.
"Buster," said Roger, "you always listen to my troubles.
You are the best listener in this house."
"I am?" thought Buster. He wagged his tail.
Then he had an idea.

Buster listened all around the room.

He listened,

and listened,

and listened.

At last he heard a tiny munching sound
coming from the dresser.
He gently poked his nose into an open drawer.
There was Maxie the hamster.
"Good dog, Buster!" cried Roger.
"You are amazing!"

Buster and Phoebe
Meet the Garbage Bandit

One night something dug through the garbage cans.
The next morning Roger said, "What a mess.
Buster! Phoebe! Bad dogs!
No biscuits for you two today!"

"We didn't do it!" barked Phoebe.

"I want my biscuit!"

But Roger did not understand.

"Phoebe," said Buster, "if we catch the garbage bandit, then Roger will know we didn't do it."

"And I can get my biscuit," added Phoebe.

After supper Buster and Phoebe hid
near the garbage cans and kept watch.
Late into the night Buster heard a sound.
Skitch, skitch, skitch.
"Phoebe, listen!" he said.
"I don't hear anything," she said.
Skitch, skitch, skitch.
"There it is again," said Buster.
"Do you hear it now?"
"No!" said Phoebe. "Now be quiet."
"Phoebe doesn't hear very well," thought Buster.

He squinted into the darkness.
A dark shape waddled across the lawn.

"The Garbage Bandit!" cried Buster.
He jumped up. "BARK ARK ARK ARK ARK!"
"Buster! Wait!" cried Phoebe.
"Can't you see it's a . . .

SKUNK?!"

But it was too late.

The skunk turned and raised its tail.

Buster yelped and leapt back.

His eyes stung.

He rubbed his nose on the grass.

"Pew-ee! You stink!" said Phoebe.

"Pew-ee! You stink!" said Roger.

"Come on, you need a tomato juice bath."

"You don't see very well," said Phoebe.
"Let *me* catch the Garbage Bandit."

The next night
Buster watched Phoebe
try to catch the Garbage Bandit.

But Phoebe did not catch the Garbage Bandit.

"You didn't *hear* him," said Buster.
"And you didn't *see* him!" said Phoebe.
"I think," said Buster, "it will take my good ears *and* your good eyes to catch that bandit."

That night Buster listened with his good ears and Phoebe watched with her good eyes.

They did not catch the skunk.

They did not catch the cats.
But they *did* catch . . .

the Garbage Bandits—all three of them!

"Good job, Buster and Phoebe!" said Roger.

Now both Buster and Phoebe
guard Roger's house.
They guard it from
everything Phoebe sees . . .

And they guard it from everything Buster hears.